SECRET SEVEN MYSTERY

The Seven are hunting for a girl who has run away from home, and use their ingenuity in following up all the clues. Jack's naughty sister, Susie, plays her usual tricks on the Seven, but in spite of her their quest has a happy ending.

Enid Blyton's

SECRET SEVEN
MYSTERY

Galaxy

CHIVERS PRESS
BATH

First published 1957
by
Hodder and Stoughton
This Large Print edition published by
Chivers Press
by arrangement with
Enid Blyton Limited
2000

ISBN 0 7540 6098 5

British Library Cataloguing in Publication Data

Blyton, Enid
  Secret Seven Mystery. —Large print ed.
  1. Secret Seven (Fictitious characters)—Juvenile fiction
  2. Children's stories 3. Adventure stories. 4. Large type books
  I. Title
  823.9'12[J]

ISBN 0-7540-6098-5

Printed and bound in Great Britain by
REDWOOD BOOKS, Trowbridge, Wiltshire

CONTENTS

CHAPTER ONE

SOMETHING INTERESTING

Peter and Janet were having breakfast with their father and mother one lovely spring morning. Scamper, their golden spaniel, was lying as usual under the table.

'Dad,' began Peter, but his mother frowned at him.

'Your father is reading the paper,' she said. 'Don't bother him just now!'

His father put down the paper and smiled. 'Do the Secret Seven want to make themselves really useful?' he asked. 'Because I've just read something in my paper that may be right up their street!'

'Oh, Dad—what?' cried Peter, and Janet put down her egg-spoon and looked at him expectantly.

'It's about a girl who's run away from home,' said their father, looking at his paper. 'She stole some money from the desk of her teacher, but when the police went to see her aunt about it, she ran away.'

'But—what can the Secret Seven do about it?' asked Peter, surprised.

'Listen—I'll read you the piece,' said his father, and propped the paper up in front of him again. 'Elizabeth Mary Wilhemina Sonning, after being accused of stealing money from the desk of her teacher, was found to be missing from her aunt's house. She took nothing with her but the clothes she was wearing, and is in school uniform and school hat. It is stated that her parents are abroad, and that she has a brother who is at present away in France.'

Peter's father looked up from the paper. 'Now comes the bit that might interest *you*,' he said. 'Elizabeth was seen on the evening of that day in Belling Village, and it is thought that she might be going to her grandmother, who lives not far off.'

'Belling Village! Why that's the next village to ours,' said Janet. 'Oh—you think that the Secret Seven could keep a look-out for Elizabeth, Daddy! Yes—

2

we could! What's she like?'

'There's a photograph here,' said her father, and passed the paper across. 'Not a very good one—but in her school uniform, which is a help.'

Peter and Janet stared at the picture in the paper. They saw the photograph of a merry, laughing girl a little older than themselves, with a mass of fluffy hair round her face. They thought she looked rather nice.

Though she can't be really, if she stole money and then ran away, thought Janet. She turned to her father. 'Whereabouts in Belling Village does her granny live?'

'It doesn't say, does it?' said her father, reaching for his paper again. 'You'll have to read this evening's paper and see if there are any more details. If the child goes to her granny's she'll be found at once, of course. But if she hides somewhere around the place, you might be able to spot her.'

'Yes. We might,' said Peter. 'The Secret Seven haven't had *anything* interesting to do lately. We'll call a meeting tomorrow. Good thing it's

3

Saturday!'

That evening, Janet sat down to write notices to each of the Secret Seven to call them to a meeting the next day. Each notice said the same things.

'Dear S.S. Member,
'A meeting will be held tomorrow morning, Saturday, at ten sharp, in the shed. Wear your badges and remember the password.'

Peter signed each one, and then he and Janet fetched their bicycles and rode off to deliver the notices, Scamper trotting beside them. They felt pleasantly excited. This new affair might not come to anything—but at least it was something to talk about and to make plans for.

'We'd better buy an evening paper on our way back and see if there's anything else in it about Elizabeth Mary Wilhemina Sonning,' said Peter.

So they stopped at the little newsagent's shop and bought one. They stood outside the shop, eagerly

4

looking through the pages for any mention of the runaway girl. At last they found a small paragraph, headed 'MISSING GIRL'.

'Here it is,' said Peter, thrilled. 'Look, Janet, it says, "Elizabeth Sonning is still missing, and her grandmother states that she has not seen her. Anyone seeing a child whose appearance tallies with the following description is asked to get in touch with the police." Then, see, Janet, there's a good description of her. That's fine— we can read it out to the Seven tomorrow.'

'Good!' said Janet. 'Come on, Scamper—we'll have to bike home pretty fast, so you'll have to run at top speed!'

Scamper puffed and panted after them, his long silky ears flopping up and down as he ran. He wasn't a member of the Secret Seven, but he certainly belonged! No meeting was complete without him.

'What's the password, Peter?' asked Janet, as they put their bicycles away. 'It's ages since we had a meeting.'

5

'It's a jolly good thing *I* never forget it,' said Peter. 'I shan't tell it to you—but I'll give you a hint. Think of *lamb*—that ought to remind you!'

'Lamb?' said Janet, puzzled. 'Well—it reminds me of sheep, Peter—or Mary had a little lamb—or lamb chops. Which is it?'

'None of them!' said Peter, grinning. 'Have another shot, Janet—and tell me at the meeting tomorrow!'

CHAPTER TWO

KNOCK—KNOCK

'Have you remembered the password yet?' asked Peter next morning, when Janet and he were tidying their shed ready for the meeting.

'No, I haven't,' said Janet. 'And I think you might tell me, because you know jolly well I've got to come. I've been thinking of lamb—lamb—lamb for ages, but it doesn't remind me of anything except what I've already told you. Tell me the word, Peter, do!'

'No,' said Peter firmly. 'You're always forgetting. It's time you were taught a lesson. I shan't let you into the meeting unless you remember it. Look—go and ask mummy if we can have some of those biscuits she made last week.'

'Go yourself,' said Janet, crossly.

'I'm the head of the Secret Seven,' said Peter. 'Obey orders, Janet!'

Janet went off, not feeling at all pleased. She was quite afraid that Peter *wouldn't* let her into the meeting! He was very strict about rules.

She went into the kitchen, but mummy wasn't there. Some lamb chops lay on the table, and Janet looked at them frowning. 'Lamb! Oh dear—whatever ought you to remind me of? I simply can't think! Oh—here's mummy. Mummy, *may* we have some of your ginger biscuits, please? Oh, what's that you've got? Mint—let me smell it. I love the smell. I wouldn't mind mint scent on my hanky!'

'It's for mint sauce with the chops,' said mummy. 'Now I'll just—'

'Mint sauce! Of *course*! That's the password, Mint sauce! What an idiot I am!' said Janet. Then she grew serious and looked solemnly at her mother.

'I shouldn't have said the password out loud! We're not supposed to tell a soul. Mummy, don't remember it, will you?'

'What are you gabbling about?' said her mother, and went to get her tin of ginger biscuits. 'Here you are—you can have all of these. I'm making some more for tomorrow.'

'Oh, *thank* you!' said Janet, delighted, and skipped off down the garden with the tin. As she came near the shed she shouted out to Peter.

'Mint sauce, mint sauce, mint sauce!'

'Have you gone mad?' said a cross voice, and Peter looked out of the shed, frowning. 'Shouting out the password for everyone to know! I'm glad you've remembered it at last.'

'Well, mummy came in with mint to make mint sauce. Wasn't it lucky?' said Janet. 'Oh, Scamper, you know I've got some ginger biscuits, don't you? I expect there'll be one for you. Peter it's almost ten o'clock.'

'I know,' said Peter. 'I'm just ready. Are there enough things to sit on? You'll have to sit on that big flower-pot, Janet. The gardener must have taken our seventh box.'

Scamper began to bark. 'That's someone coming already,' said Peter. 'Shut the door, Janet, please. We'll have to ask the password as usual.'

Knock—knock!

'Password!' called Peter.

'Mint sauce!' said two voices.

'Enter!' said Peter, and Janet opened the door. 'Hello, George and Colin. You're very punctual.'

Knock—knock.

'Password!' shouted Peter. A cautious voice came in through the keyhole.

'I've forgotten. But I'm Pam, so you can let me in.'

'No, we can't. You know the rule,' said Peter, sternly.

'Think of lamb chops!' called Janet, before Peter could stop her.

A giggle was heard. 'Oh, yes—of course. MINT SAUCE.'

9

Janet opened the door, but Peter looked quite cross. 'How dare you remind Pam like that?' he demanded.

'Well, *you* reminded me!' said Janet, indignantly. 'You said, "Think of lamb chops", didn't you?'

'There's someone else coming,' said Peter, changing the subject hurriedly.

Knock—knock! 'Mint sauce,' said two voices.

'Come in!' shouted Peter, and in came Jack and Barbara together. Scamper greeted them with pleasure, and then everyone sat down and looked expectantly at Peter.

'Anything exciting?' asked Jack, eagerly.

'Yes—quite,' answered Peter. 'But what about that awful sister of yours, Jack? Is she anywhere about? This is quite an important meeting.'

'No. She's gone shopping with my mother,' said Jack. 'She doesn't even *know* there's a meeting on. So we're quite safe. She won't come snooping round.'

'Have a ginger biscuit?' asked Janet, and the tin was handed round.

Peter cleared his throat. 'Well, now,'

he began, 'it was my father who thought we should inquire into the matter I'm going to tell you about, so you can see it's quite important. It concerns a girl who has run away from her aunt's home, after stealing some money at school. She's been seen near here, at Belling Village, where her grandmother lives—but so far hasn't been to see her granny.'

'Oh—and I suppose it's up to the Secret Seven to keep a look-out for her—and find her!' said Jack. 'We ought to be able to do *that* all right. What's she like—and what are your plans, Peter?'

'That's just what this meeting is about,' said Peter. 'Now listen!'

CHAPTER THREE

MOSTLY ABOUT ELIZABETH

Peter explained everything clearly.

'The girl's name is Elizabeth Mary Wilhemina Sonning,' he said. 'Her parents live abroad, and she is a weekly boarder at school and spends her week-ends with an aunt. She has a brother who is away in France. She was accused of stealing money from her teacher's desk, and when the police went to speak to her aunt about it, she ran away.

'What was she dressed in?' asked Pam.

'School uniform,' said Peter. 'Here's her photograph in it. Ordinary navy school coat, navy felt hat with school band round it, ordinary shoes, and socks. It says here that she wore a grey skirt underneath, with a white blouse—well, really she's dressed just like Janet and Pam and Barbara when they're at school, it seems to me!'

'She might have taken some other clothes with her,' said Jack. 'Her Sunday coat or something.'

'No. Her aunt said that no other clothes were missing—only the ones she went in,' said Peter.

'You may be sure the aunt would look carefully, because it would be difficult to spot the girl if she were not in her school uniform.'

'Where's the description of what she's like?' asked Janet. 'It was in the evening paper last night, Peter.'

'Oh yes. Here it is,' said Peter, and began to read out loud. ' "Elizabeth—can be recognised by her mass of soft, dark, curly hair, her brown eyes, straight eyebrows, and scar down one arm. She is tall for her age, and strong. She swims well and is fond of horses." Well—there you are—do you think you'd spot her if you saw her?'

'We might,' said Colin, doubtfully. 'But lots of girls have dark, curly hair and brown eyes. If only the girl would wear short sleeves we might spot the scar—but that's the one thing she will certainly hide!'

'How do we set about looking for her?' asked George. 'Do we bike over to Belling Village and hunt all over the place?'

'That's what we've got to discuss,' said Peter. 'I don't actually think that just biking up and down the streets is going to be the slightest good—Elizabeth will be sure to find a hiding-place. She won't wander about in the

13

daytime, I imagine—she'll lie low.'

'Where?' asked Pam.

'How do *I* know?' said Peter, who thought that Pam was sometimes very silly. 'Use your brains, Pam. Where would *you* hide if you ran away from home?'

'In a barn,' said Pam.

'In the woods under a thick bush,' said George.

'Wuff, wuff, wuff-wuff,' said Scamper, wagging his tail.

'What did you suggest—in a *kennel*?' said Peter. 'Thank you, Scamper— quite a good idea of yours.

Everyone laughed, and Scamper looked pleased.

'I thought it would be sensible if we thoroughly explored Belling Village and round about,' said Peter. 'If Elizabeth has already actually been *seen* in Belling, she must be hiding *somewhere* near. I expect the police have already hunted pretty well everywhere, but we know better where to look than they do—because we know where *we'd* hide if we wanted to—but they wouldn't. Grown-ups seem to forget the things they did when they were young.

'Yes, they do,' said George. 'But I *never* shall. I'm determined not to. What about the grandmother, Peter? Should one of us go to see her, do you think? She might have something helpful to say.'

'Yes, I think that's a good idea,' said Peter, considering it.

'Bags *I* don't go,' said Pam, at once. 'I wouldn't know what to say. I should just stand there and look silly.'

'Well, you'd find *that* quite easy,' said Colin, and Pam scowled at him.

'Now just you tell me what you—' she began, but Peter stopped the argument before it began.

'Shut up, you two. Jack and I will go, probably. And listen—there is another thing we might do.'

'What?' asked everyone.

'Well, this girl is fond of horses, it seems. We might go to the two or three stables we know of and see if any girl has been seen hanging around. She might even try to get a job at one.'

'That's a *good* idea,' said Janet,

15

warmly. 'Well—there seems quite a lot we can do, Peter.'

'The next thing is to give each one of us a section of the countryside to hunt,' said Colin. 'It's no good us all going together—for one thing anyone in hiding would hear us coming and lie low. And for another thing we'd never cover all the countryside! What particular places must we search, Peter?'

'Well—you'll use your own common sense about that, of course,' said Peter. 'Anywhere that looks likely—a deserted shack—an empty caravan—a copse—anywhere in the woods where there are thick bushes—barns—sheds—even a hen-house!'

'Wuff, wuff, wuff-wuff,' put in Scamper.

'You mentioned a kennel before, Scamper, old thing,' said Peter. 'We'll leave *you* to examine those. Now, Secret Seven, there are two hours before dinner. Arrange between yourselves where you're going to search. Jack and I are going off to the grandmother's house. Everyone report back at half-past two—SHARP! Now—get going!'

CHAPTER FOUR

JUMBLE FOR MRS SONNING

Peter and Jack went out of the shed together. 'Do you know the address of the grandmother?' asked Jack.

'No, I don't,' said Peter. 'But I know her name is Sonning, the same as the girl's—so I vote we look it up in our telephone book.'

'Good idea,' said Jack. 'We'll get our bikes afterwards.' The two boys went down the path to the garden door, and Peter looked for the telephone book. He found it and began to hunt for the name of Sonning.

'What are you looking for, dear?' asked his mother, coming into the hall. 'Can't you find a number?'

'I was looking for the phone number of that runaway girl's grandmother,' said Peter. 'But she's not on the phone

17

apparently.'

'But Peter, dear—you can't telephone her house and ask her questions about her granddaughter!' said his mother, quite shocked.

'I wasn't going to, Mother,' said Peter. 'I was going to call there with Jack—but I don't know her address.'

'I know it,' said his mother, surprisingly. 'She often runs jumble sales for Belling Women's Institute, and it was only last week that she wrote and asked me for some old clothes.'

'Some jumble?' said Peter, excited. 'Oh, Mother—what a chance for us! Can't we take some over to her, and say it's from you—and maybe she'll tell us a lot about Elizabeth, her granddaughter. We're looking for her, you know, just as Daddy suggested.'

'Oh dear—you and your Secret Seven!' said his mother. 'Very well— I'll give you some jumble, and you can say I've sent it by you. But you're to be polite and kind, and if she doesn't want to say a word about Elizabeth, you are NOT to ask questions.'

'All right, Mother. We'll be quite

polite, really we will,' said Peter. 'Where's the jumble?'

'In those two boxes,' said his mother. 'I dare say you can strap them on the back of your bicycles if they won't go into your baskets. The address is "Bramble Cottage, Blackberry Lane".'

The two boys hurried off jubilantly with the jumble. 'Wasn't that a bit of luck?' said Peter. 'Come on—we've got a wonderful excuse for calling on the old lady!'

They rode off with Scamper running beside them, panting. They soon came to Belling Village, and asked for Blackberry Lane.

It was a little winding lane, with fields on one side and a wood on the other. Bramble Cottage was the last house in the lane, a pretty little place with tulips and wallflowers in the garden, and creepers climbing up the whitewashed walls.

'Here it is,' said Peter, seeing the name on the gate. 'Get your jumble, Jack.'

They carried the two cardboard boxes up the path, and rang the bell beside the green front door. They heard footsteps coming, and then someone in an overall opened the door and looked inquiringly at them.

She couldn't be the grandmother, Peter was certain. She looked a good deal too young.

'We have brought some jumble for Mrs Sonning's sale,' he said. 'May we speak to her, please? I have a message from my mother.'

'Come in,' said the woman, and led the way to a small sitting-room. 'Put the boxes down there, please. You can't see Mrs Sonning—she's in bed, not very well. I'm Miss Wardle, her companion, and *I'll* tell her you brought these.'

'I suppose she's very upset about her granddaughter,' said Peter, plunging in at once. 'My mother was sorry to hear about it too.'

'Ah, yes—the old lady is very troubled,' said Miss Wardle. 'She's so fond of Elizabeth, and is longing for the child to come to her. She doesn't believe all that nonsense about stealing money. Neither do I!'

20

'Do you know Elizabeth, then?' asked Peter.

'Know her! I've known her since she was so high!' said Miss Wardle. 'And a nicer, more honest, straightforward child I've never seen. A bit of a rascal at times, but none the worse for that. Poor child—I can't bear to think of her hiding away somewhere, afraid to come out.'

'Do you think she's somewhere about here?' asked Jack. 'She has been seen in the district, hasn't she?'

'Yes—and, what's more, it's my belief she's been here, to this very house!' said Miss Wardle, lowering her voice. 'I haven't told Mrs Sonning about it, it would worry her. But some of my tarts went last night and a meat pie—and a tin of biscuits! And a rug off the backroom sofa!'

This was news indeed! Peter looked at Jack. Elizabeth must certainly be in the district!

'Why do you suppose she won't come to her grandmother and stay with her instead of hiding away?' asked Peter. 'People usually hide when they feel guilty. But you say you don't believe Elizabeth *is* guilty of stealing that money!'

'That's true—I don't,' said Miss Wardle. 'But the pity of it is—the money was found in her chest of drawers! So what are you to believe?'

'Who's that, Emma, who's that?' a voice suddenly called from upstairs. 'Is there any news of Elizabeth?'

'That's Mrs Sonning. You must go,' said Miss Wardle, and ran up the stairs at once.

'Come on,' said Peter to Jack. 'We've got quite a lot of information! And on Monday we'll see if there's any more! I'll find another boxful of jumble, Jack—and we'll bring it to Miss Wardle and see if she has anything more to report—maybe another rug gone, or a pie! Come on, Scamper—we've done well!'

CHAPTER FIVE

PAM AND BARBARA ARE BUSY

Now how had the others been getting on? Well, Pam and Barbara had been having a very busy time. They had planned to explore the woods and the fields on the east side of Belling, while the boys and Janet explored the rest of the countryside—or as much as they could!

'There's an old shed on that field, look,' panted Barbara, as she toiled up a hill on her bicycle. 'Let's go and see if it looks as if someone is camping there.'

They left their bicycles by a gate and climbed into the field. The shed was in good repair—and the door was locked!

'Hm,' said Pam. 'Locked! I wonder why. Field sheds aren't usually locked. How can we look inside, Barbara?'

'There's a tiny window this side,' reported Barbara. 'But too high up to peep through. Let's look through the keyhole.'

There was nothing whatever to see through the keyhole, for the inside of the shed was pitch dark. It would have to be the window or nothing! Pam fetched her bicycle from the gate and proposed to stand on the saddle while Barbara held it steady. She was just about to stand on the saddle when a loud shout made her lose her balance in fright and fall off.

'Hey, you! What are you doing?'

The two girls turned round and saw a farm labourer leading a horse towards them. Pam couldn't think of any excuse but the truth.

'We—we were only just wondering what was in the shed,' she stammered. 'We weren't doing any harm.'

'Well, that's the shed where I lock up my tools,' said the man. 'Little nosy-parkers! Get off this land before I call the police!'

The girls left that field at top speed. Pam riding her bicycle over the bumpy clods! Gosh—what a cross person!

'We'd better be careful of the next shed we want to look into,' said Pam, as they cycled along. 'Look, there's an empty caravan—see, in that field there. That would be a good place for anyone to hide in. Now for goodness' sake let's be careful this time. I'll keep guard while you look inside. Hurry up!'

Pam stood on guard near the dirty, broken-down old caravan, which looked as if no one had lived in it for years.

Barbara went cautiously up the steps and looked inside.

She beckoned to Pam in excitement.

'Pam! Someone *does* live here! There are a couple of dirty old rugs— or blankets—and a tin mug and plate— do come and look!'

Pam came up the steps too. 'Pooh!' she said, and held her nose. 'What a DREADFUL smell! Come down, Barbara. You know jolly well you'd never hide in a place like that, nor any other schoolgirl either. I think I'm going to be sick.'

'You're right, I'd rather sleep in a ditch than in there,' said Barbara. 'Don't be sick, Pam. It's not worth it. Come on, let's get on with our job. We

25

want to have plenty to report to the others this afternoon.'

Pam decided not to be sick after all, and they rode on again, keeping a sharp eye out for any kind of hiding-place. But except for a roadman's hut, they saw nothing else that was possible to hide in. They didn't even stop at the little hut, because the roadman himself was there, sitting in it and having some kind of snack.

'What about the woods?' asked Pam, at last. 'There's Thorney-Copse Wood—and it has plenty of thick bushes in it. We might go there. We've still got an hour to look round in.'

So they went to the nearby woods, and left their bicycles beside a tree. 'Now let's be as quiet as possible,' said Pam, in a low voice. 'You go that way, and I'll go this. Whistle twice if you see anything interesting.'

She went quietly in and out of the trees, looking behind any thick bush and even under them. But there was nothing at all interesting or exciting to be seen. Pam found an empty cigarette packet, and Barbara found a dirty handkerchief with J.P. on it, but neither of them felt that they were of any value in the hunt. Now if E.M.W.S. had been marked on the handkerchief, what a thrill!

And then Pam suddenly clutched hold of Barbara, making her jump violently, and hissed in her ear. 'Quiet! Somebody's coming, and it's a girl—look!'

They crept under a thick bush at once, and made little peep-holes through the leaves. Yes, it was a schoolgirl—in navy blue coming down a path towards their bush.

'Keep still—and then we'll follow her!' whispered Pam. 'I bet that's the girl we want!'

The girl's hat was pulled well down over her eyes. She walked boldly up to the bush—and then suddenly fell into it, almost squashing Pam and Barbara. She began to roar with laughter.

'Oh, it's SUSIE. Jack's horrible sister Susie!' cried Barbara, indignantly. 'Get off us, Susie—you've nearly squashed us flat. What did you do that for?'

'Well, you were lying in wait to jump

out at me, weren't you?' asked Susie. 'I spotted you crawling into the bush!'

'We were *not* lying in wait for you,' said Pam.

'Well,' said Susie, what were you doing then? Come on—you've *got* to tell me!'

CHAPTER SIX

UP AT THE STABLES

Pam and Barbara glared at Susie. It was *just* like her to interfere. Pam rubbed her shoulder.

'You've given me a big bruise,' she said. 'And we shan't tell you a thing!'

'It's something to do with the Secret Seven, isn't it?' said Susie. 'Go on, tell me—I know it is. You've got some kind of secret on again, haven't you? Jack has gone off without saying a word to me. Tell me, and I'll help you.'

'Certainly not!' said Pam indignantly. 'We keep our secrets to ourselves!'

'Well—I'll get it out of Jack,' said the

irritating Susie, and walked off, tipping her hat over her face once more. 'Good-bye—and don't lie in wait for me again!'

'Now she knows we're in the middle of another excitement,' said Barbara, brushing herself down. 'She's so sharp that I'm sure she'll find out what it is. I do hope we don't keep meeting her looking for Elizabeth too!'

'Time's getting on,' said Pam, looking at her watch. 'We'll just hunt in a few more places, and then we'll have to go home!'

They did quite a lot more hunting, and found an exciting hollow tree which, they decided, would have made a fine place for a runaway girl if she had happened to see it.

'We'll remember it for ourselves, in case we ever need a place like this,' said Barbara. 'Now let's go home. We've nothing to report—except about Susie—but at least we've done our best. I wonder how Colin got on? He was going round the farms and looking into the barns.'

'And George and Janet were going to

visit the riding stables in the district,' said Pam. 'That would be quite a nice job. I love stables.'

George and Janet thought it was quite a nice job too. They had looked up the riding stables in the district, and found that there were three.

'Belling Riding Stables,' said Janet. 'And Warner's Riding Stables—and Tiptree's. We'll go to all three, shall we?'

So off they went on their bicycles, feeling, as usual, very important to be on Secret Seven work again. They came to Tiptree's Stables first. Janet knew the man who ran it, for he was a friend of her father's.

He was rubbing down a horse and smiled at Janet and George. 'Well—come to have a look at my horses?' he said. 'I've a foal in there, look—Silver Start, she's called, and a bonny thing she is.'

They admired the lovely little foal. 'I do wish I worked at a stables,' said Janet, artfully. 'Do you ever let schoolgirls work here—perhaps in the school holidays, Mr Tiptree?'

30

The riding master laughed. 'No! I get plenty of help from my wife and two daughters—they're all mad about horses. They do all the work there is to do—I don't need anyone from outside. This is quite a family stables! Why—did you think you'd come and help? Your father has surely got plenty of horses for you to play about with?'

'Well, yes, he has,' said Janet, stroking the little foal. 'I only just wondered if you ever gave jobs to girls—lots of girls I know love horses and wish they could work in stables.'

'Come on, Janet,' said George, seeing that they could get no useful information from Mr Tiptree. Obviously the runaway girl would not be able to get a job here, even if she wanted one.

'Thank you for showing us the foal, Mr Tiptree,' said Janet. 'I'll tell my father about her—he'll be interested.'

They rode off again, and George looked at his list of stables. 'We'll go to Warner's Stables next,' he said. 'That's not far from the old granny's house. It might be a good place for Elizabeth

Sonning to hide in—or get a job at.'

'I hardly think she'd go anywhere so close, would she?' said Janet. 'She might be recognised. It's more likely she'd go farther off—to Belling Stables, the other side of the village. Still—we'll go to Warner's first.'

They rode up to the stables on the top of the next hill. Below them were spread fields of all kinds and shapes looking like a big patchwork quilt.

Warner's Stables was quite big, and looked busy as they came up to it. Some horses were going out with riders, and others were coming in. Nobody took much notice of the two children.

'Let's have a snoop round,' said Janet. 'And if we see any stable-girls, we'll have a good look at them.'

'Wouldn't Elizabeth have to wear riding things if she wanted a job at a stable?' said George. 'We know that she was wearing her school clothes when she left—she took no others.

'Well—she might have borrowed some at the stables,' said Janet. 'Though that's rather unlikely, I think.

32

Look—there's a stable-girl—see—cleaning out that stable.'

They stood and stared at the girl. Her back was towards them, and she was doing her job well. She turned round to fetch something, and at once they saw that it was not Elizabeth.

'Far too big!' said Janet, disappointed. 'Look—there are two stable-boys over there. Let's go and talk to them—we may learn something, you never know.'

CHAPTER SEVEN

TOM HAS SOME NEWS

George and Janet made their way between the horses and their riders to where the two stable-boys were. One was carrying a great load of straw on his back. The other was helping a small girl down from a pony. They took no notice of George and Janet.

'Hello, Janet!' said the small girl, and Janet turned in surprise. It was Hilda, a little girl who went to her school, and was two years below her.

'Hello, Hilda,' said Janet, feeling pleased to see her. Now she could pretend she was with her, and it wouldn't matter that she and George were not in riding clothes. Everyone would think they had come to meet Hilda.

'Thank you, Tom,' said Hilda to the boy who had helped her down. He took the pony off to a nearby stable, Hilda followed him, accompanied by Janet and George.

'I like the other boy best,' Hilda said. 'He talks to me, but this one won't. Come and see me give my pony some sugar. He's a darling.'

They walked over to the stable with her, following Tom and the pony. The other lad had gone into the same stable with his straw, and was now spreading it on the floor of a stall. He whistled as he worked, and had a merry look in his eye.

'You talk to this boy, and I'll talk to the other one,' said George, in a low voice to Janet. 'Talk to Hilda too—find out if any new girl is here helping in any way—or if she has seen any strange girl wandering about, watching, as we are doing.'

'Right,' said Janet, and went to Tom and Hilda.

'It must be fun working with horses,' she said to the boy, who was now fastening the pony to the wall. He nodded.

'Not bad,' he said.

'It's funny that so many more girls ride than boys,' went on Janet. 'I can't see a single boy here except you, and the other stable-boy. Are there any others?'

'No,' said the boy. 'Just us two.' He began to clean out the stall next to the little pony, turning his back on Hilda and Janet. Janet thought he was rather rude. So did Hilda.

'He's like that,' she whispered to Janet. 'The other boy, Harry, doesn't mind telling you anything. He's talking to George as if he's known him for years.'

So he was. George was getting on very well indeed!

'Do they have many stable-girls here?' George asked, when he had a good chance. The burly fellow shook his head.

'Only one—and she's over there. One came the other day to ask for a job, but Mr Warner turned her down at once. Why, she wasn't any bigger than you! And yet she said she could handle this big cob over there.'

George pricked up his ears. He wasn't interested in the cob, but he was interested in this girl who had come for a job? Could it have been Elizabeth?

'What was she like?' he asked. Harry called across to the other stable-boy.

'Hey, Tom—what was that girl like who came and asked for a job the other day?'

'Was she brown-eyed?' asked George, eagerly. 'Had she masses of dark, fluffy hair? And did you notice if she had a scar down one of her arms?'

The stable-boy swung round sharply and stared at George. 'What girl's that?' he asked. 'Is she a friend of yours?'

'No, not exactly,' said George. 'It's—

36

er—well, it's just someone we're looking out for. Do tell me, was this girl like my description of her?'

'I didn't see her,' said Tom, much to Janet's and George's disappointment. 'I wasn't here the day she came.'

'Oh, no—that's right,' said Harry. 'Well, I know she hadn't got dark hair—she had yellow hair, and she was lively as a monkey. Very cross too, when Mr Warner turned her down. She couldn't have been your friend.'

'I saw a girl like the one you described when I was in Gorton the other day,' said Tom suddenly. 'Mass of fluffy brown hair, you said, didn't you—and a scar down one arm.'

'Did you? Did you *really* see her?' cried Janet, coming up, looking thrilled. Now they were really getting warm! 'How did you manage to see her scar?'

'Oh—she sat in a tea-shop, and it was hot there—so she took off her coat,' said Tom. 'I saw her scar then.'

'But hadn't she a long-sleeved school blouse on?' asked Janet, surprised.

'Maybe. But her sleeves must have

been rolled up if so,' said Tom, and bent to his work again.

'Tom—this is really very important,' said George, joining in. 'Could you tell us anything she said—did she speak to you?'

'She said she was going to catch a train to London and see if she could fly to France to join a brother of hers,' said Tom, to Janet's and George's surprise and excitement. Why, the girl *must* have been Elizabeth, then. A scar on her arm—and a brother in France! There was no doubt about it!

'Tom! I want you!' called a voice, and Mr Warner looked into the stable. 'Come and show this child how to saddle her horse.'

Tom went off, and Janet and George looked at one another, delighted. 'Well—we've got something to report to the meeting this afternoon!' said Janet. 'Come on, George—we needn't stay here any longer.'

CHAPTER EIGHT

ANOTHER MEETING

Everyone was early for the two-thirty meeting, and the password was muttered five times as Janet and Peter opened and shut the door of the shed. Scamper barked a welcome to everyone. Then the door was locked and the meeting began.

'I hope everyone has something to report,' said Peter. 'I'll begin with my report. Well, Jack and I went to the grandmother's house, but the old lady wasn't well, so we didn't see her. We didn't find it difficult to ask questions, and her companion was quite friendly.'

'That was a bit of luck!' said George.

'It was,' said Peter. 'We learnt quite a few things—for instance, that Elizabeth is definitely hiding somewhere in the district—not far from her granny's, I should think—because she has got into the house at night and taken pies and things, and an old rug!'

George and Janet looked astonished. 'But, Peter—' began George and Janet together. Peter frowned. 'Please don't interrupt,' he said. 'You and Janet can have your say in a minute. Well, as I was saying—the old lady's companion, Miss Wardle—told us quite a lot about Elizabeth, and said that she was a very nice, straightforward girl.'

She can't be!' interrupted Pam. 'You can't call a thief straightforward! She was only just *saying* that!'

'Be quiet,' said Peter, exasperated. 'The point I'm trying to make is that there's no doubt that Elizabeth is hiding somewhere near her grandmother's—and getting food from there. And she'll do that at night as often as she needs food! I suggest that we go and watch one night, and see if we can catch her. Jack and I are going to take some more jumble to the grandmother's on Monday, and if Elizabeth has been getting into the house again, we could perhaps watch that night.'

'Yes. Jolly good idea!' said Pam,

Barbara, and Colin. George and Janet said nothing, but looked meaningly at one another.

'Well, that's my report—mine and Jack's,' said Peter. 'What about you, Colin?'

'Nothing to report at all,' said Colin, in a rather apologetic tone. 'I examined about six sheds, all kinds of barns, and wandered over a whole caravan colony the other side of Belling Hill—but didn't find out a thing. Not a thing. I'm sorry, Peter.'

'That's all right,' said Peter. 'You and Pam, Barbara—what's your report?'

'Well, nothing much, either,' said Barbara. 'We looked in a locked shed—or tried to—and got turned off by a man with a horse. And we found a terribly smelly old caravan with a rug inside and a tin cup and plate. And we hunted all through Thorney-Copse Wood, looking into and under bushes.'

'And that awful sister of Jack's was there, too,' said Pam. 'We saw her coming along, dressed in the same uniform as we wear—navy blue coat and hat—and we thought it might be

41

the runaway girl, so we hid in a bush—
and Susie jumped right into it on
purpose and fell on top of us—you
should see the bruise I've got!'

'So *that's* why Susie was pestering the
life out of me at dinner to find out
what the Secret Seven are up to!' said
Jack. 'You *are* a couple of idiots to
make her think there is something up,
you two. Now I shan't have a moment's
peace. Susie is bound to find out what
we're after—she's as sharp as a needle.'

'She certainly is,' said Peter, who had
a healthy respect for Susie's sharpness.
'I wouldn't be a bit surprised if she's
not snooping outside somewhere now,
listening for all she's worth.'

'Scamper would bark,' began
Janet—and just at that very moment
Scamper *did* bark as a face looked in at
the window of the shed! It was Susie, of
course.

'Hello, Secret Seven,' she called. 'I
thought you'd be here, Jack. I know
what you're all up to. I found your
newspaper cutting! Ha, ha.'

Peter looked furiously at Jack.
'Do you mean to say you left that

42

newspaper report about?'he said.

'That's right, tick him off!' said the annoying Susie, pressing her face closer to the window. 'Hey, you do look a lot of sweetie-pies sitting down there. Shall I tell you my news of Elizabeth Mary Wilhemina Sonning?'

Jack leapt up in a fury, flung open the door, and raced out with Scamper at his heels. The others went to the door.

Susie was a fast runner. She was running out of the gate, laughing, before Jack was half-way there. He knew it was no good chasing after her. He went back to the shed, red in the face.

'Do you suppose she heard what we were all saying?' asked Jack. Peter shook his head.

'No. Scamper would have barked. Susie could only just that moment have come. I must say it's very annoying. Now Susie will be hunting too. Bother! If she finds Elizabeth before we do, I shall be jolly furious.'

'She won't, said George, bursting to tell what he had heard from Tom the

43

stable-boy. 'You just wait till you hear what Janet and I have to report.'

CHAPTER NINE

REPORTS AND PLANS

'Give your report, George and Janet,' said Peter. 'It sounds as if it may be an important one.'

'It is,' said Janet, proudly. 'You begin, George.'

'Well,' began George, 'Janet and I went to Tiptree Stables first, but as they don't employ anyone there except their own family, we knew Elizabeth wouldn't have got a job there. So we left at once and went on to Mr Warner's stables.'

'And we saw a stable-girl there, but she was much too big to be Elizabeth,' put in Janet.

'Then we saw two stable-boys—one a big, burly fellow called Harry, and the other smaller, called Tom. He was a bit surly, we thought, but Harry wasn't. He

44

was nice. We asked him if any girl had been asking for a job at Mr Warner's, and one had, but she had yellow hair not brown, so we knew that was no good.'

'And when we told Harry what the girl was like that we wanted, the other boy, Tom, who was listening, suddenly said that *he* had seen a girl like the one we were describing—and she even had a scar down one arm!' cried Janet unable to resist joining in.

'What!' cried everyone, and sat up straight.

'This *is* news,' said Peter, delighted. 'Go on, George. Where had he seen Elizabeth—because it must be her if the description tallies.'

'He said he met her in a tea-shop in Gorton—that's not very far from here, is it? She was having tea, I suppose. It was hot and she had her coat off— that's how he noticed the scar down one arm. She talked to him.'

'What did she say?' demanded Peter, his eyes shining.

'She told him she was going to London to see if she could get a plane to fly to France to see her brother,' said Janet. 'She did really! So it *must* have been Elizabeth, mustn't it?'

'Yes. Of course it must,' said Peter, and the others nodded their heads. A brother in France—a scar on one arm—it could *only* be Elizabeth.

'Well, now you see why Janet and I don't think that Elizabeth is hiding anywhere in the district,' said George. 'She's probably hiding somewhere in London, trying to find out about planes.'

'Well—can you answer this question then, if that's so,' said Peter, looking suddenly puzzled. 'If Elizabeth is in London, waiting to fly to France, who is it who is taking pies and a rug from her grandmother's house at night?'

There was a deep silence. Everyone looked at Peter, even Scamper.

'I hadn't thought of that,' said Janet. 'Well, of course, George and I didn't know anything about the pies till you told us in your report, Peter. Bother! One of our reports is wrong somehow. If Elizabeth is hanging round her granny's house at night, she can't be going to fly to France!'

'She might have found that she hadn't enough money to get to London and buy a seat on a plane,' said Jack. 'She might have changed her mind and gone to Belling, after all. She might even have hoped to get money from her grandmother's house. After all, if she had stolen once, she could easily do so again.'

'That's true,' said Peter. 'Yes—I think you're right, Jack. She may have made that plan at the beginning and then found she hadn't enough money—and so she came to this district. We know she was seen somewhere about here.'

There was another silence. The Seven were trying to sort things out in their minds. 'What about that girl who came to ask Mr Warner for a job—the one Harry told you about,' said Janet to George. 'He said she had golden hair, didn't he? Well, I suppose she might have had it dyed, mightn't she—I mean, that *might* have been Elizabeth, after all. I know my auntie once had her hair dyed golden when it was

47

brown. So Elizabeth could have done the same, couldn't she?'

Nobody knew very much about hair being dyed, and Peter made up his mind that the next thing to do was to go and interview the two stable-boys himself. They might be able to tell him something they hadn't thought of telling Janet or George.

'I shall go and see those boys,' he said. 'What are they like to look at?'

'I told you Harry was big and burly, and the other smaller,' said George. 'They've both got dark hair, rather untidy. They ought to exchange riding-breeches too—Harry's are too small for him, and Tom's are too large! Wasn't it a bit of luck Tom meeting Elizabeth at Gorton—now we know for certain she must be somewhere about, still wearing her school things.'

'Well, she's *got* to be somewhere near, or she couldn't raid her granny's house at night,' said Peter. 'Now, what do we do next? Tomorrow's Sunday, we can't do anything then. It will have to be Monday after school.'

'You and I will go to old Mrs

Sonning's with some more jumble,' said Jack, 'and find out the latest news from *that* quarter.'

'And after that we'll go and see the stable-boys,' said Peter. 'The others can come too, so that it won't seem too noticeable, us asking questions. Meet here at five o'clock on Monday. Well— I *hope* we're on the trail—but it's not very easy at the moment!'

CHAPTER TEN

MISS WARDLE HAS MORE NEWS

Sunday passed rather slowly.

When Peter and Janet came back from morning church, Peter had an idea.

Janet—George and I are going to take some more jumble to old Mrs Sonning tomorrow, you remember—to make an excuse for asking about Elizabeth again—so shall we hunt up some? What sort of things does Mother give for jumble? Old clothes mostly, I suppose.'

'Yes. But we can't give away any of our clothes without asking her,' said Janet. 'And she would want to know why we were doing it—she'd guess it was an excuse to go to old Mrs Sonning again, and she might not approve.'

'That's just what I was thinking,' said Peter. 'I know—let's turn out our cupboards and see if there's anything we can find that would do for jumble.'

They found plenty! It was astonishing what a lot of things they had which they had quite forgotten about and never used.

'Two packs of snap cards,' said Peter. 'A game of snakes and ladders—we've never even *used* it, because we always preferred our old game. And look here—a perfectly new ball! Shall we give that?'

'Well, jumble isn't really supposed to be *new* things,' said Janet. 'Let's give our old ball instead. And look, here are my old sandals I thought I'd left at the seaside! I can't get into them now—*they* can go.

In the end they had quite a big box

full of jumble and felt very pleased with themselves. They longed for Monday to come!

It came at last, and then there was morning school to get through, and afternoon school as well. They raced home to tea and were down in the shed just before five o'clock. All the Seven were there, very punctual indeed!

'Good,' said Peter, pleased. 'Well, Jack and I will bike to Bramble Cottage, and see if we can get any more news out of Miss Wardle, the companion, or Mrs Sonning, the granny. The rest of you can bike up to Warner's Stables and wait for us there. Chat to the stable-boys all you can. We'll join you later.'

They all set off, Peter with a neat box of jumble tied to the back of his bicycle. They parted at the top of Blackberry Lane, and Jack and Peter went down the winding road, while the others rode up the hill to where Warner's Stables were, right at the top.

Peter and Jack left their bicycles at the gate of Bramble Cottage and went to the front door. They knocked, hoping that Miss Wardle would come, not old Mrs Sonning. Mrs Sonning might not be so willing to talk about Elizabeth as Miss Wardle was!

Thank goodness it was Miss Wardle who opened the door again. She seemed quite pleased to see them.

'Well now—don't say you've been kind enough to bring us some *more* jumble!' she said. 'Mrs Sonning was *so* pleased with the boxes you brought on Saturday. I'll give her these—she's still in bed, dear old lady.'

'Oh, I'm sorry,' said Peter. 'Hasn't she heard any more of her granddaughter?'

'Not a word,' said Miss Wardle. 'The police say she seems to have disappeared completely—and yet she came here again last night—*and* the night before!'

This was indeed news! 'Did she?' asked Peter eagerly. 'Did you see her? Did she leave a note?'

'No. Not a note, not even a sign that she was here,' said Miss Wardle, 'except that more food was gone. How she got in beats me. Every door and window I made fast myself. She must have got a key to the side-door. That's the only one with no bolt.'

'What do the police say about that?' asked Jack.

'Nothing,' said Miss Wardle, rather indignantly. 'It's my belief they think I'm making it up, they take so little notice. Why don't they put a man to watch the house at night—they'd catch the poor child then, and what a relief it would be to the old lady to know she was safe!'

'They probably *do* put a man to watch,' said Peter, 'but I expect Elizabeth knows some way into the house that they don't. I bet she knows if there's a policeman about—and where he is and everything. *I* would! Why don't you watch, Miss Wardle?'

'What? Watch every door and window?' said the companion. 'Nobody could do that. And I'm not one to be able to keep awake all night, even if I had to.'

'Well—we'd better go,' said Peter. 'I *do* hope Elizabeth is soon found. It must be awful hiding away in some cold, lonely place all by herself, not daring to come home because she feels ashamed.'

They said good-bye and went. 'Well,' said Peter, as soon as they were out of the front gate, 'I know what *I'm* going to do tonight! I'm going to hide somewhere in the garden here! I bet I'll see Elizabeth if she comes—but I shan't tell the police. I'll try and get her to go and tell everything to her granny!'

'Good idea! I'll come too!' said Jack, thrilled. 'Let's go up to the stables now and find the others. I bet they'll want to come and watch as well!'

CHAPTER ELEVEN

TOM—AND A BIT OF EXCITEMENT

Peter and Jack saw the others as soon as they pushed open the tall double-gate and went into the big stable-yard. They had evidently been sent to fetch hay and straw, and looked very busy indeed, carrying it over their shoulders.

The two stable-boys were there as well, helping.

'Hallo, Peter—hallo, Jack!' called Janet. 'Aren't we busy? We're having a lovely time. Mr Warner said we could take the ponies down to the field later on, with Harry and Tom, the stableboys.'

'Good. I'll come too, with Jack,' said Peter, pleased. He loved anything to do with horses, and often helped old Jock, the horseman, in his father's farm-stables. He went over to the two stable-boys. Harry grinned at him, but Tom just nodded. Peter looked at him keenly. So this was the boy who had actually seen Elizabeth!

'Hey—I hear you saw that girl, Elizabeth Sonning, at Gorton the other day,' began Peter.

'That's very interesting. The police haven't found her yet—I should think her grandmother must be feeling ill with worry, wouldn't you?'

'What about the girl, then?' said Tom, in a gruff voice. 'I reckon she must be feeling pretty awful too.'

'Well, if she stole that money, she

55

deserves to feel awful,' said Peter. 'The funny thing is that Miss Wardle, who is the old lady's friend, says Elizabeth is an awfully nice girl, straightforward as anything! Here—let me help you with that saddle.'

'Thanks,' said Tom. 'I feel interested in that girl—seeing her in Gorton just by chance. I reckon she's in France by now. She said she wanted to go to her brother.'

'Well, she's *not* in France,' said Peter, struggling with the heavy saddle. 'She goes each night to her granny's house and takes things. Miss Wardle told me that. She says she can't *think* how Elizabeth gets into the house— everything's locked and fastened. She thought maybe the girl might have a key to the side-door, which has no bolts.'

Jack joined in then. 'And we thought we'd go and watch the house ourselves tonight,' he said. 'We're sure *we* should see her getting in, if she comes in the dark—and we'd try and get her to go and talk to her old granny, who loves her. We hate to think of a girl camping out somewhere all alone, feeling miserable.'

'Are you really going to watch tonight?' said Tom, sounding surprised. Peter nodded. He hadn't wanted Jack to tell a Secret Seven plan to the stable-boy—that was really *silly* of him, thought Peter, and gave him a stern frown, which startled Jack very much.

'Well, if you're going to watch the house, I'd like to come too,' said Tom, most surprisingly. 'I bet *I* could see anyone creeping into a house at night. I'll come with you.'

Peter hesitated. He wanted to say that Tom could certainly *not* come! But how could he prevent him if he wanted to? It was just a nice little adventure to him, and possibly a chance to show how clever he was at spotting anyone breaking into a house!

'All right,' he said, at last. 'We shall be there at half-past ten. I'll give an owl-hoot when we arrive—and if you're there, hoot back.'

'I'll be there,' said Tom. 'And I suppose a policeman or two will, as well! Well, you stick up for me if I get seen by the police, and say I'm a friend of yours, not a burglar!'

'All right,' said Peter, wishing more than ever that Jack hadn't said so much. 'Do we take the ponies down to the fields now?'

Apparently they did, and a long trail of children riding or leading ponies went over the hill and down to the fields, bright in the evening sun.

After they had safely fastened in the tired ponies, the Seven, with Tom and Harry, walked back to the stables. Tom looked tired and spoke very little. Harry cracked jokes and slapped the other stable-boy on the back several times. Peter whispered to Tom when he had a chance.

'Don't forget the owl-hoot!' Tom nodded and turned away. The children shouted good-bye and fetched their bicycles, riding them down the hillpath.

In the distance they saw someone climbing over a stile—someone with a suitcase—someone in a navy blue coat and hat—someone who looked round and then, seeming scared, ran hurriedly down the road.

'Look!' said Colin, pointing. 'Is that Elizabeth—with a suitcase, too! Quick, let's follow!'

They rode along the path, bumping up and down as they went, for it was very rough. They came to the stile. By it lay something white.

Janet picked it up. 'A handkerchief!' she said. 'LOOK! It's got E in the corner, embroidered in green! It *was* Elizabeth! Her hiding-place *is* somewhere near here. Quick, let's follow her.'

They lifted their bicycles over the stile into the road and looked to see if they could spy a running figure in navy blue.

'There she is—at the corner—by that old cottage!' shouted George. 'If only we can get her to be friends and come with us! Ring your bells, all of you, so that she'll hear us coming!'

CHAPTER TWELVE

HOW VERY ANNOYING!

The whole Seven cycled as fast as they could after the disappearing figure in navy blue, ringing their bells loudly to attract her attention.

The figure reached the corner, and vanished round it. When they came to it, the girl was nowhere to be seen. The Seven dismounted from their bicycles and looked at one another.

'Wherever has she gone? She's nowhere down the road!' said Janet. 'She must have slipped into some hiding-place. But I can't see any near by.'

'Yes, look—there's that ruined old cottage,' said Colin, pointing. 'Can't you see it—among that little thicket of trees. I bet she's there!'

'We'll go and look,' said George, and, putting their bicycles beside the hedge, they squeezed through a gap and ran over to the old stone cottage.

It had very little roof left, and there were only two rooms below and one above. A broken stone stairway went up in one corner to the room above.

'There's nobody here!' said Pam, surprised. 'Oh, but look—there's an old stone stairway. Perhaps she's up there!'

George ran up—and gave a shout. 'The girl isn't here—but her suitcase is! And it's got E.M.W.S. on it! It *was* Elizabeth we saw!'

Everyone tore up the stairs in a hurry. They looked at the cheap little suitcase on the dirty floor. Yes—it certainly had E.M.W.S. printed on it in black.

'Elizabeth Mary Wilhemina Sonning,' said Barbara, touching the initials. 'But where *is* Elizabeth?' she called loudly. 'Elizabeth! Where are you?'

There was no reply. 'That's odd,' said Janet. 'There really isn't anywhere for her to hide here. Why did she throw her case up these stairs and then rush away. She might guess we'd find it. Where *is* she? ELIZABETH!'

'I'm going to open the case,' said Peter. 'I feel there's something peculiar about all this. I hope it isn't locked.'

It wasn't. It snapped open easily enough. The Seven crowded round to look inside. One small box was there, and nothing else. It was tied up with string.

'Perhaps this is the money she stole!' said Colin. 'Gosh—look! It's got "THE MONEY" printed on it in big letters. Open the box, Peter.'

Peter undid the string and opened the box. Inside was a smaller one, also tied with string. He undid that, and inside found once again another box. He looked puzzled. It seemed strange to put money inside so many boxes!

He opened the third box—and inside that was a card, laid on its face. Peter picked it up and turned it over. He stared at it as if he couldn't believe his eyes!

'What does it say? What does it say?' cried Pam, trying to see.

Peter flung it down on the floor and stamped on it, looking very angry. 'It says *"Lots and lots of love from Susie!"* Oh! I'd like to slap her! Making us chase after her—leaving that silly hanky by the stile—and making us undo all those boxes!'

The Secret Seven were very, very angry, especially Jack. 'How *dare* she play a trick like that!' he said. 'Just wait till I get home. I'll have something to say to her!'

'Where's she gone?' said Barbara. 'I didn't see her after we turned the corner. She must have had her bicycle hidden somewhere here.'

'She planned it all very well,' said George.

'I must say she's jolly clever. Gosh—I really *did* think we'd got hold of Elizabeth that time!'

'Susie must have laughed like anything when she printed the initials E.M.W.S. on that cheap old suitcase,' said Jack. 'I recognise it now—it's been up in our loft for ages.'

'Well, come on—let's get home,' said Janet. 'I'm tired of talking about Susie.'

They left the little ruined cottage and rode away. Peter began to arrange the night's meeting with George, Jack, and Colin. The girls were sad that they could not come too.

'You always leave us out of these night adventures,' complained Janet. 'I do so wish we were coming. It will be so exciting to wait in that dark garden—let me see—there will be five of you counting that boy Tom—though I really do think it's a pity to have him, too.'

'There may be a policeman or two as well,' said George. 'I vote we get there before they do—or they'll get rather a shock when they hear a whole collection of people taking up their positions here and there in the garden!'

Everyone laughed. 'Don't you DARE to let anything out to Susie about tonight,' Peter warned Jack. 'We can't have her ruining everything. I do wonder how Elizabeth gets into the house. She must have an extra key.'

They arranged to meet at ten past ten at the corner and bicycle all together to Belling. 'We'll hide our bikes under the nearby hedge and get into the garden at the back,' planned

Peter. 'Remember to hoot if there's any danger.'

'This is awfully exciting,' said Jack. 'I only hope Susie doesn't hear me getting up and going downstairs.'

'Jack—if you do anything silly so that Susie follows you, I'll dismiss you from the Secret Seven!' said Peter—and he REALLY meant it!

CHAPTER THIRTEEN

WAITING AND WATCHING

That night Peter, Jack, George and Colin slipped silently out of their houses. Jack was very much afraid that Susie might hear him, but when he put his ear to her door, he could hear gentle little snores. Good—she was asleep! He remembered Peter's threat to dismiss him from the Secret Seven if he wasn't careful about Susie, and he felt very glad to hear those snores!

The boys met together and then cycled quickly over to the

grandmother's house in Belling. They met nobody at all, not even a policeman, and were very thankful. The four of them dismounted quietly and put their bicycles into the hedge beyond Bramble Cottage. The cottage was in complete darkness.

'The only person to hoot is *me*,' whispered Peter. 'If we all hoot when we hear or see something interesting or suspicious, it would sound as if the garden was *full* of owls—and any policeman would be most suspicious!'

'All right,' whispered back George. 'Can we choose our own hiding-places? What about two of us going to hide in the garden at the front of the house, and two at the back?'

'No—two at the back, one in the front—you, Colin—and one at the side where the side-door is' said Peter, in a low voice. 'Don't forget that Miss Wardle said she thought Elizabeth might have a key to that door—and there are no bolts there on the inside!'

'Oh, yes!' said Jack. 'I'll go and hide in the hedge beside the garden door, Peter. There isn't any door on the fourth side. We shall be watching every door there is—and every window.'

'It's very dark,' said Peter, looking up at the sky. 'There's no moon, and it's a cloudy night, so there are no stars either. We shall have to keep our ears wide open, because it may be pretty difficult to see anything.'

'Our eyes will soon get used to the darkness,' said Colin. 'Hey—listen, what's that?' He clutched at Peter and made him jump.

A slight noise came from near by, and then a shadow loomed up. A voice spoke. 'It's me—Tom. I was waiting here, and I heard you. Where are you hiding?'

They told him. 'Well, I think *I'll* climb up a tree,' said Tom, in a low voice. 'That will be a very good place to watch from—or listen from! I don't think any policemen are about. I've been here for some time.'

'Hoot if you hear anyone coming,' Peter reminded him. 'I'll hoot back. But only you or I will hoot.'

'I'll find a tree to climb,' whispered Tom. 'See—that one over there, near the wall. I shall have a good view from there—if only the clouds clear and the stars shine out!'

The four went to find their own hiding-places, feeling pleasantly excited. This *was* fun! They heard Tom climbing his tree. Then there was silence. Peter was snuggled into a bush, from where he could keep good watch.

A sudden screech made everyone jump, and their hearts beat fast. Whatever was it? Then a white shadow swept round the dark garden, and everyone heaved a sigh of relief.

'Only a barn-owl!' thought Peter. 'Gosh—it made me jump. Good thing it doesn't hoot, only screeches—or we would all of us have thought that someone was coming!'

Nothing happened for a while—then a low, quavering hoot came across the garden. 'Hoo! Hoo-hoo-hoo-hoooooooo!'

'That's Tom!' thought Peter, and he and the others in hiding stiffened, and listened hard, trying to see through the darkness.

Then someone brushed by Peter's

bush and he crouched back in fright. He heard a little cough—a man's cough. It must be a policeman who had come along so quietly that no one but Tom had heard him. Peter waited a few seconds till he was sure that the man had found a hiding-place, and then he hooted too.

'Hoo! Hoo-hoo-hoo-hooooooo!'

'Now everyone must guess that at least one policeman was in the garden! Peter's heart began to thump. Suddenly things seemed very strange and very exciting—all the dark shadows around, and so many people waiting! He half hoped that Elizabeth would not come to her granny's house that night. It would be so frightening for her to be surrounded suddenly by complete strangers!

Then suddenly he stared in amazement. Was that a *light* he saw in one of the upstairs rooms of the house? A light like that made by a torch? Yes—it was! He could see the beam moving here and there behind the drawn curtains!

Elizabeth must be there—she must

have got in somehow, in spite of everyone watching! Or could it be Miss Wardle creeping about with a torch? No—surely she would switch on a light! Peter gave a hoot again. 'Hoooo! Hoo-hoo-hoo-hoooooooooo!' That would make certain that everyone was on guard. If Elizabeth had got in, then she would have to get out—and surely one of them would see her!

The light in the upstairs room disappeared—and reappeared again in another room. Peter thought it was the kitchen. Perhaps the hungry runaway girl was looking for food again?

'HOW HAD she got in? But, more important still—where was she going to come out?

CHAPTER FOURTEEN

A REAL MYSTERY!

The light from the torch inside the house moved here and there. Then it disappeared completely, as if it had been switched off. All the watchers

70

listened, and strained their eyes in the darkness. Now Elizabeth would be leaving the house, and they must stop her. What door—or what window—would she creep from?

Nothing happened. No door opened. No window creaked or rattled. For ten whole minutes the watchers stood silent and tense. Then a man's voice called from somewhere in the garden.

'Will! Seen anyone?'

To Peter's intense surprise another man's voice answered. 'No. Not a thing. The kid must be still in the house. We'll knock up Miss Wardle and search.'

So there were *two* policemen in the garden then! How very quiet the other one had been! The boys were most surprised. *Now* what should they do? They watched the policemen switch on torches and heard them go to the front door of the house.

Peter hooted once more, and the others, realising that he wanted them, left their hiding-places and came cautiously to find him. Tom slid down the tree and joined them too.

'The policemen didn't hear or see anyone—any more than we did!' said Peter. 'We could only have seen what they saw—a light in the downstairs of the house. Tom, did *you* see anything else?'

'Not a thing,' said Tom. 'Look—I'll slip off, I think. The police don't know me, and they might wonder what I'm doing here with you. So long!'

He disappeared into the night and left the four boys together. They went near to the front door, at which the policemen had rung a minute ago. Keeping in the dark shadows. The door was being opened cautiously by a very scared Miss Wardle, dressed in a long green dressing-gown, her hair in pins.

'Oh—it's you!' the boys heard her say to the police. 'Come in. I'm afraid I was asleep, although I said I'd try and keep awake tonight. Do you want me to go and see if anything is taken?'

'Well, Miss Wardle, we know that *someone* was in your house just now,' said one of the policemen. 'We saw the light of a torch in two rooms. One of us would like to come in and search,

72

please—the other will stay out here in case the girl—if it is the girl—tries to make a run for it. We haven't seen her come out—or go in either for that matter! But we did see the light of her torch.'

'Oh, I see. Well, come in, then,' said Miss Wardle. 'But please make no noise, or you'll scare the old lady. Come into the kitchen—I can soon tell if food is gone again.'

The policeman disappeared into the cottage with Miss Wardle, leaving the other man on guard in the garden. The four boys watched from the safety of the shadows. Surely Elizabeth must be in the house? She couldn't have left by any door or window without being seen or heard! They watched lights going on in each room, as Miss Wardle and the policeman searched.

After what seemed like a very long time, they heard voices in the hall. Miss Wardle came to the door with the policeman.

'Nothing to report, Will,' said the policeman to the man left on guard. 'Nobody's in the house. Miss Wardle even went into the old lady's room to make sure the girl hadn't crept in there, feeling that she was cornered.'

'Well—nobody's come *out* of the house,' said Will, sounding surprised. 'Has anything been taken?'

'Yes—more food. Nothing else,' said the first policeman. 'Strange, isn't it? How could anyone have got in under our very eyes and cars—taken food—and got out again without being heard or seen going away? Well—thanks, Miss Wardle. Sorry to have been such a nuisance for nothing. How that girl—and it *must* be the girl—gets in and out like this beats me. And where she's hiding beats me too. We've combed the countryside for her! Well—her brother's coming over to this country tomorrow—not that *he* can do much, if we can't!'

The police departed. The front door shut. The light went off in the hall, and then one appeared upstairs. Then that went out too. Miss Wardle was presumably safely in bed again.

'What do you make of it, Peter?' whispered Jack. 'Peculiar, isn't it?'

'Yes. I can't understand it,' said Peter. 'I mean—there were us four hiding here—and two policemen—and Tom up the tree—and yet not one of us saw Elizabeth getting in and out—and not one of us even *heard* her.'

'And yet she must have come here, into this garden,' said Jack. 'She broke in somewhere—or unlocked a door—she even put on her torch in the house to see what she could take—and then she got out again, with us all watching and listening—and disappeared. No—I don't understand it either.'

'Come on—let's go home and sleep on it,' said Peter. 'I feel quite tired now, with all the waiting and watching—and the excitement—and now the disappointment. Poor Elizabeth—what must she be feeling, having to scrounge food at night, and hide away in the daytime? She must be very miserable.'

'Well—maybe her brother can help,' said Colin. 'He'll be here tomorrow. Come on—I'm going home!'

CHAPTER FIFTEEN

CROSSPATCHES

The four boys belonging to the Secret Seven overslept the next morning. They were so tired from their long watch the night before! Janet was cross when Peter wouldn't wake, because she was longing to know what happened!

'Gosh—I'll be terribly late for school,' groaned Peter, leaping out of bed. 'You might have woken me before, Janet.'

'Well, I squeezed a sponge of cold water over you, and yelled in your ear, and pulled all the clothes off!' said Janet indignantly. 'And Scamper barked his head off. What *more* would you like me to do? And what happened last night?'

'Nothing. Absolutely nothing!' said Peter, dressing hurriedly. 'I mean, we didn't get Elizabeth—she got into the house, took what she wanted, and got out again—and disappeared. And

76

although there were seven people altogether in the garden, watching, nobody saw her. So you see—nothing happened. ALL RIGHT, MOTHER! I'M JUST COMING.'

He tore downstairs with his mother still calling him, ate his breakfast standing up, and then cycled to school at top speed. He yelled to Janet as he left her at the corner.

'Meeting tonight at five-thirty. Tell Pam and Barbara!'

The meeting was not very thrilling. After such high hopes of something really exciting happening the night before, everyone felt flat. Pam made them all cross by saying that if *she* had hidden in the garden she would certainly have heard or seen Elizabeth creeping by.

'You must have fallen asleep,' she said. 'You really must. I mean—*seven* of you there! And nobody heard a thing! I bet you fell asleep.'

'Be quiet,' said Peter crossly. 'You don't know what you're talking about, Pam. Now don't start again. Be QUIET!'

'Well,' said Pam, obstinately, 'all I

can say is that if Elizabeth *really* didn't get in or out, and it seems like that to me, or you'd have heard her—then she must be hiding in some secret place *inside* the house.'

'The police searched all over it,' said Peter. 'I did think of that bright idea myself—but I gave it up when the policeman hunted all through the cottage last night without finding Elizabeth. After all, it's only a small place—no cellars—no attics. We did hear *one* thing of interest, though. The brother who's in France is arriving in this country today. Maybe he'll have something to say that will be of help.'

'Well—why don't you go and see him, then?' said Pam, who was in a very persistent mood that day. 'You could tell him what *you* know—about Tom the stable-boy seeing Elizabeth in Gorton, for instance.'

'H'm. That's the first sensible remark you've made, Pam,' said Peter. He turned to Jack. 'Will you come with me, Jack? I'd like to see the brother, I must say.'

'Wuff-wuff-wuff!' said Scamper,

suddenly.

'*Now* what's the matter?' said Peter, whose late night had made him decidedly impatient that day. 'What's Scamper barking for? If it's Susie I'll have a few sharp words to say to her about playing that stupid trick on us with the suitcase!'

It *was* Susie. She stood grinning at the door when Peter opened it. 'Mint Sauce!' she said promptly. 'Let me in. I've some clues—great big ones. I know where Elizabeth is and what she's doing. I . . .'

'You do NOT!' yelled a furious Peter, and called for Jack. 'Jack get her out of here! Pam, Barbara, Janet—get hold of her dress and pull, too. Come on! Get going!'

And for once in a way the cheeky Susie was taken by surprise and found herself being dragged to the gate, and not very gently either!

'All right!' she yelled, kicking and hitting out as vigorously as she could. 'I shan't tell you my big clues. But you'll see I'm right! And I know your password, see! Mint sauce, Mint sauce,

79

Mint sauce!'

She disappeared up the lane, and the Seven went back to the shed, feeling better for the excitement. 'Now we shall have to alter our password,' said Peter, in disgust. 'How did Susie know it, Jack? Have you been saying it in your sleep, or something?'

'No,' said Jack, still angry. 'She must have hidden somewhere near the shed and heard us saying it. Bother Susie! You don't think she really *does* know something, do you?'

'How can she?' said Peter. 'And why can't you keep her in order? If Janet behaved like that I'd give her a piece of my mind.'

'You would *not*,' said Janet, indignantly. 'You just try it!'

'Gosh—we really are crosspatches today!' said Barbara, surprised. 'The boys must be tired after their late night! Well—have we any plans?'

'Only that Jack and I will go and see Elizabeth's brother, if he's arrived at the grandmother's,' said Peter, calming down. 'He'll be sure to go there, because his sister is known to be somewhere near. Come on, Jack—I'm fed up with this meeting. Let's go!'

CHAPTER SIXTEEN

UNEXPECTED NEWS

Peter and Jack arrived at Bramble Cottage on their bicycles, and at once heard voices there. They put their cycles by the gate and looked over the hedge.

Three people were sitting in deck-chairs in the little garden, enjoying the warm evening sunshine. One was Miss Wardle—one was an old lady, obviously the grandmother—and one was a youth of about eighteen, looking very worried.

'He must be the brother,' said Peter. 'Good, he's arrived! Come on. We'll go up the front path, and if Miss Wardle sees us, she'll call us and we'll go over and talk.'

Miss Wardle did see them, and recognised them at once. 'Oh,' she said to the old lady beside her, 'those are the two nice boys who brought all that jumble. Come here boys—I'm sure Mrs Sonning would like to thank you.'

Peter and Jack walked over. 'Good evening,' said Peter, politely. 'I do hope you have news of your granddaughter, Mrs Sonning.'

'No. We haven't,' said the old lady, and to Peter's alarm, a tear rolled down her cheek. 'This is my grandson, Charles, her brother. He's come over from France to see if he can help, because Elizabeth is very fond of him. If she knows he is here, she may come out of hiding.'

'We met a boy the other day who saw her in Gorton,' said Peter. 'She must have been on her way here then.'

'What!' said the boy Charles. 'Someone actually saw her in *Gorton*! But that's *not* on the way here. Who was this boy?'

'One of the stable-boys up at Warner's Stables there,' said Peter, pointing up the hill. 'He said Elizabeth told him she was going to France to see you.

'But she didn't know where I *was* in France,' said Charles. 'I've been travelling around all the time! Even the police only got in touch with me with great difficulty! I'm certain that Elizabeth wouldn't have been mad enough to try to find me when she didn't even know what part of France I was in!'

'Well,' said Peter, 'that's what *Tom* said she told him, and he couldn't very well have made it up, because he had never met her before!'

'I'll go and see him,' said Charles, and got up—but just then the telephone bell shrilled out, the noise coming clearly into the garden.

'Answer it, Charles, there's a dear,' said old Mrs Sonning, and the boy went indoors. Peter and Jack waited patiently for him, and were immensely surprised to see him come running out again at top speed, his eyes shining and his face aglow.

'Granny! It was Elizabeth's headmistress. She . . .'

'Oh—has the child gone back to school—or gone back to her aunt?'

83

said the old lady.

'No! But all that upset about the stolen money is cleared up!' said Charles, taking his grandmother's hand. 'It *wasn't* Elizabeth who took it, of course. The girl who stole it got frightened when the papers kept reporting that Elizabeth hadn't been found, and she suddenly owned up.'

'Who *was* the girl?' said Miss Wardle, indignantly.

'I'm afraid it was the one supposed to be Elizabeth's best friend,' said Charles. 'Lucy Howell—she came here to stay with Elizabeth last year, Granny. She saw the cash-box in the desk and took it on the spur of the moment, without even opening it. She hid it somewhere, waiting for a chance to break it open. She didn't realise that there was about a hundred pounds in it, and she was horrified when the police were called in about it.'

'I should think so!' said Mrs Sonning. 'I never did like Lucy—a sly little thing I thought she was. I was sorry that she was Elizabeth's friend.'

'Well, apparently Lucy was annoyed

84

with Elizabeth and very jealous of her just then, because Elizabeth was ahead of her in marks and doing better at games—and what did she do but take the cash-box and put it into Elizabeth's chest of drawers! When the boarders' trunks and chests were searched—Elizabeth is a weekly boarder as you know—the cash-box was found—still unopened! Elizabeth had gone home for the weekend to Aunt Rose's, and the police went there to question her.'

'Poor Elizabeth!' said Mrs Sonning. 'But didn't she deny taking the money?'

'Yes, of course—but she wasn't believed. Most unfortunately she had actually been in the classroom where the money had stupidly been left, doing some homework all by herself, and had been seen there. Aunt Rose was very upset—and poor Elizabeth felt there was nothing to do but run away! I expect she thought she might have to go to prison or something!'

'Poor child! But now she can come back with her name cleared!' said Mrs Sonning. 'What a dreadful thing to happen to someone like Elizabeth. She's as honest as can be.'

'Yes. But how are we going to let her know that everything is all right?' asked Miss Wardle. 'We don't even know where the child is!'

'No. That's true,' said Charles, worried. 'But we *must* find her! She took only enough money with her to pay her railway fare down here apparently—that's all she had. She wouldn't have enough to buy food or anything else. She's hiding somewhere, all alone worried and miserable—thinking that we're all ashamed of her!'

'Don't,' said old Mrs Sonning, and began to weep into her handkerchief. 'Such a dear, good child—always so kind. Charles, we must find her—we must!'

'Well—the first thing to do is for me to go up and see this stable-boy who met Elizabeth in Gorton,' said Charles, getting up. 'Will you take me up to him, you two boys?'

'Yes,' said Peter and Jack, who had been listening to the conversation with much interest. 'We'll take you now. We are so glad everything's cleared up!'

CHAPTER SEVENTEEN

A FUNNY BUSINESS ALTOGETHER

Peter, Jack, and Charles went to the gate at the bottom of the little garden, and up the hill to Warner's Stables, the two boys wheeling their bicycles. They liked Charles. He reminded them of someone, but they couldn't think who it was.

'Where's Tom?' Peter called to Harry, when they came to the stables. He was saddling a horse.

'Somewhere about,' he shouted back. 'Over there, I think.'

'You see if Tom is over there, and I'll go into the stables and see if he's there,' said Peter. Charles went with Jack, and Peter looked into the stables. At the far end he saw Tom, cleaning out one of the stalls.

'Hey, Tom!' called Peter. 'There's

someone wants to see you.'

'Who?' shouted back Tom.

'You remember meeting that girl Elizabeth?' said Peter. 'Well, it's her brother, Charles. He's come over from France, he's so upset, and . . .'

He stopped, because Tom had suddenly flung down his rake, and had shot past him at top speed. He tore out of the door, and Peter stared in surprise. When Peter got to the stable door himself, there was no sign of Tom! He saw Jack and Charles coming towards him, and called to them.

'Did you see Tom? He tore out of here just now, goodness knows why!'

'We saw someone racing off,' said Jack. 'Bother! Just as we wanted him. Didn't you tell him someone wanted to see him?'

'Yes, of course. I don't know if he heard me or not, but he suddenly flung down his fork and dashed off without a word!' said Peter, puzzled.

Harry, the other stable-boy, came up with the big stable-girl. 'Don't take any notice of Tom,' he said. 'He's a bit odd! Isn't he, Kate?'

The stable-girl nodded. 'Hasn't got much to say for himself,' she said. 'Funny boy—a bit potty, I think!'

'But where did he go?' said Peter. 'Do you know where he lives? We could go to his home, and then our friend here could ask him a few things he wants to know.'

Neither Harry nor the girl knew where Tom lived, so Jack and Peter gave it up. 'Sorry,' they said to Charles and Peter added: 'We could come here again tomorrow if you like. Not that Tom can really tell you anything of importance. He may even have made it all up about meeting Elizabeth. He may have read about her in the papers, and just invented the whole meeting! He really *is* a bit odd, I think.'

'Well—thank you,' said Charles, who looked worried again. 'I'll go back. My poor old granny won't be herself again till we find Elizabeth. My parents haven't been told yet, but they'll have to be rung tomorrow, and asked to come home. Dad's out in China on a most important job, and we didn't want to worry him at first. Apparently the police thought they would soon find my sister.'

'Yes—with no money—and wearing her school clothes it *ought* to have been easy to spot her,' said Jack. 'Well—good-bye—and good luck!'

The boys rode off down the hill. 'I'm really glad Elizabeth didn't steal that money after all,' said Peter. 'Though we've never met her, I thought it was rather strange that anyone said to be so honest and straightforward should have done such a thing. And now I've seen that old granny, and her nice brother Charles—he *is* nice, isn't he, Jack?—I see even more clearly that Elizabeth couldn't have been a thief.'

'It's a funny business altogether,' said Jack. 'And it's not cleared up yet, Peter—not till Elizabeth's found. Remember, *she* doesn't know that the real thief has owned up!'

'I know,' said Peter. 'Well—we'll have another Secret Seven meeting tomorrow night, the same time as today, Jack. We'll tell the others at school tomorrow. We'll have to report this evening's happenings, and see if there's anything further we can do.'

'Right!' said Jack. 'See you tomorrow!' and with a jingling of bicycle bells the two parted, each thinking the same thing. 'What a pity Elizabeth doesn't know that her name is cleared!'

Next evening the Secret Seven gathered in the meeting shed as usual, anxious to hear what Jack and Peter had to say. They were all very thrilled to hear about the brother Charles— and the exciting telephone call that had come while Jack and Peter were there.

'What a pity that boy Tom didn't stop and speak to Charles,' said Colin, puzzled. 'Do you suppose he made up that tale about meeting Elizabeth, and was afraid of being found out in his fairy-tale by Charles?'

'*I* tell you what!' said George, suddenly. 'I believe he knows where Elizabeth is! That's why he acts so strangely! That's why he ran off like that—to warn her that her brother was there!'

'You may be right, George,' said

Peter, considering the matter. 'Yes—perhaps he *does* know where she is! Well—all the more reason why we should go up tomorrow and see him! We'll ask him straight out if he knows where the girl is—and watch his face. He's sure to give himself away if he *does* know where she is—even if he swears he doesn't!'

'We'll tell Charles to come too,' said Jack. 'If *he* thinks Tom knows his sister's hiding-place, I've no doubt he'll be able to make him tell it!'

'Right,' said Peter. 'Well—tomorrow may be exciting. We'll just see!'

CHAPTER EIGHTEEN

PETER GOES MAD

The next evening the Seven took their bicycles and went riding to Warner's Stables once more, leaving a message at Bramble Cottage for Charles to follow, if he wished. He was out when they called.

Harry and the stable-girl were carting straw about the yard, but Tom was nowhere to be seen.

'He asked if he could work down in the fields today,' said Harry. 'Not in the stables. You could bike down to them, if you want him. He's a bit touchy today, is old Tom!'

'If someone called Charles comes along, tell him where we are,' said Peter. 'That's the boy who was with us yesterday.'

They rode down to the fields, and saw Tom in the distance exercising ponies round the meadow. They shouted to him and waved.

He stopped and looked hard at them all. Then he waved back and came cantering over.

'Sorry I'm busy,' he said. 'Is there anything you want?'

'Yes!' said Peter, putting his bicycle by the gate and climbing over the top bar. 'Tom—I want to ask you a question. Do you know where Elizabeth Sonning is hiding? *Do* you?'

A frightened look came into Tom's face. 'Why should I know that?' he said. 'Don't be crazy!' And with that he kicked his heels against the pony's side and galloped off!

'He does know! He does!' said Jack. 'And he won't tell.' He turned to Peter and looked suddenly astonished. 'Why, Peter—what on earth's the matter? Why are you looking like that?'

Peter did indeed look peculiar—astonished—bewildered—as if someone had knocked him on the head. Jack shook him, quite scared.

'Peter! What is it?'

'Gosh—of *course* he knows where Elizabeth is!' said Peter. 'Nobody in the world knows better where Elizabeth hides out! Nobody!'

'Peter!' cried everyone, wondering if he had suddenly gone mad. What in the world did he mean?

He didn't answer, but did something very surprising. He lifted his bicycle over the gate into the field, mounted it and rode over the grass after Tom, who was still cantering along, on the pony.

The Seven stared open-mouthed. No doubt about it—Peter had gone off his head! Now he was shouting at the top of his voice.

'Come here, you idiot! Everything's all right! Elizabeth! COME HERE! I've got good news for you! Elizabeth! ELIZABETH!'

'Mad,' said Jack, looking quite scared. They all stood and watched, really amazed.

Now Peter was cycling quite near to Tom and his rather frightened pony, and he was still shouting.

'Everything's all right, I tell you! Lucy Flowell confessed *she* took the money! Everyone knows it wasn't you! WILL you stop, you idiot, and listen to me?'

And at last the pony stopped, and the rider allowed Peter to cycle up and jump off by its side. The six by the gate poured into the field to hear what was happening.

Peter was out of breath, but he still talked. 'You're Elizabeth! I know you are! I *knew* your brother reminded me of someone—and I suddenly saw the likeness just now at the gate! Elizabeth, it's all right. Your name's cleared. And

95

look—there's your brother at the gate. Come now—you *are* Elizabeth, aren't you?'

Tears began to fall down the girl's face. 'Yes—I *am* Elizabeth Sonning! Oh, is it true that Lucy said she took the money? I thought she had—but I wasn't sure. Nobody will think me a thief any more?'

'Nobody,' said Peter. 'Well, you're a brave kid, aren't you—getting a job as a stable-boy, and working hard like this! Where did you hide at night? How . . . ?'

'Oh—there's Charles!' cried Elizabeth, suddenly, though the Seven still couldn't help thinking of her as Tom, of course! The girl galloped her pony over to Charles, shouting to him: 'Charles! Charles! Oh, I'm so glad to see you!'

She almost fell off her pony into his arms, and the two hugged one another tightly. The Seven went over to them, feeling excited and pleased. What a surprising ending to the problem they had been puzzling over so long!

'Well, you monkey!' said Charles,

who suddenly looked much younger. 'What have you got to say for yourself? Bringing me over from France like this—having everyone hunting for you? Where have you been hiding? How did you get in and out of Granny's house? Why . . . ?'

'Oh, Charles—I'll answer all your questions!' said Elizabeth, half-crying and half-laughing. 'But let's go to Granny's, do let's. I do want to hug her, I do want to tell her everything's all right!'

'Come on, then,' said Charles, putting his arm round his sister. He turned to the Seven. 'You kids can come too,' he said. 'We've a lot to thank you for—and I'm longing to know how you spotted that this dirty, untidy, smelly stable-boy was no other than my naughty little sister Elizabeth.'

CHAPTER NINETEEN

A JOLLY GOOD FINISH

They all went out of the field, and took the path that led down to Bramble Cottage. The Seven were very thrilled to be in at the finish. To their great disgust they met Susie on her bicycle, riding along with a friend.

'Hallo!' she called cheekily. 'Solved your silly mystery yet?'

'Yes!' said Jack. 'And that boy Tom was Elizabeth—dressed up like a stable-boy. *You'd* never have thought of that in a hundred years!'

'Oh, but I knew it!' said the aggravating Susie. 'Shan't tell you how! But I knew it!' And away she went, waving her cheeky hand at them.

'She's a terrible fibber,' said Janet. 'I suppose she *couldn't* have guessed, could she, Jack?'

'I wouldn't put it past her,' said Jack, with a groan. 'Anyway, she'll keep on and on saying she knew. *Why* did I tell her just now?'

'Goodness knows,' said Peter. 'You'd better safety-pin your mouth, Jack! Well—here we are at the cottage. Won't the old granny be pleased?'

She was! She hugged the brown-faced, short-haired girl and kissed her, happy tears streaming down her face.

Miss Wardle rushed indoors and brought out biscuits and lemonade for everyone. Scamper, who was there as usual, of course, was delighted to have two fine biscuits presented to him.

'Elizabeth! Now where did you hide? And are those *my* riding-breeches?' asked Charles, pulling at them. 'Where did you get them?'

'From your chest of drawers here,' said Elizabeth. 'I knew nobody would miss them. They're rather big for me, though. And I've made them very dirty! I hid in the hayloft at the stables each night, with just a rug to cover me. I was quite warm and cosy.'

'So you *did* take that rug!' said Miss Wardle. 'I thought so! And all that food too, I suppose?'

'Yes. You see, I'd no money left after

paying my fare down here,' said Elizabeth. 'At least, I had five pence, that's all. So I had to get a job—but you're only paid once a week, so I had to have food till my wages were due—I couldn't go without eating!'

'You poor child!' said Miss Wardle. 'Bless you, I knew you were innocent, I knew you weren't a thief! Yes, and I cooked special tarts and pies for you, my little dear, and left them out, hoping you'd come and take them.'

'Oh—thank you!' said Elizabeth. 'I did wonder why there was such a *lot* of food in the larder—and food I especially liked!'

'Why did you tell us that you had met—well, met *yourself* in Gorton, and all that?' asked Peter, puzzled.

'Only to put you off the scent,' said Elizabeth. 'I thought if people imagined I was off to France to find Charles, they wouldn't guess I was hiding near Granny's. I had to come near Granny's because of getting food, you see—and, anyway, I wanted to *feel* I was near somebody belonging to me, I was so miserable.'

'How did you get into the house, Elizabeth?' said Miss Wardle, and Charles chimed in with:

'Yes—how did you?'

And Peter added, 'Why, the other night we all watched here in the garden—but, how very funny, you were here too, Elizabeth, pretending to watch for yourself—you were Tom, up that tree! *Were* you up the tree?'

Elizabeth laughed. 'Yes, of course. That tree has a branch that goes to the bathroom window—and I know how to open the window from the outside and slip in—I'll show you, it's quite easy if you have a pocket-knife. But I'm getting too large to squeeze through it now, really! It really made me laugh to think of everyone watching and waiting—and there was I, up the tree, waiting to slip through the window. I got a lovely lot of food that night—did you see my torch shining in the downstairs rooms? And I was just sliding down the tree again when I heard the police knocking on the front door.'

'And you told us not to tell the police

you were there—because you knew your pockets were full of food!' said Peter, with a chuckle. 'Yes, I think your brother's right. You really are a monkey.'

'But I was a very, very good stable-boy,' said Elizabeth, earnestly. 'Granny, Mr Warner said he was very pleased with me, and he even promised me a rise in wages if I went on working so hard! Can I go on being a stable-boy? It's nicer than being at school.'

'Certainly not!' said her grandmother, smiling. 'You'll go back to school and be welcomed there by everyone—and you'll work hard and be top of the exams, although you've missed a week and a half!'

'But what *I* want to know is—how did *you*, Peter, realise so suddenly that Tom the stable-boy was Elizabeth?' asked Charles.

'Well—I suddenly saw the likeness between you,' said Peter. 'And then somehow the bits of the jigsaw all fell into place, if you know what I mean! And I was so afraid that Elizabeth would run off again when she saw you, as she did when she heard you were at the stables yesterday, that I just felt I had to cycle at top speed after her pony and yell at her!'

'I was never so surprised in my life as when you came at me and my pony at sixty miles an hour on your bike, yelling at the top of your voice,' said Elizabeth. 'But I'm glad you did. Granny, I'm coming here for the holidays, aren't I? Can I have these children to play sometimes?'

'Of course!' said her grandmother. 'I shall always be glad to see them. There's only one thing I'm sad about Elizabeth—your hair! *What* a pity you hacked it short like that. It was so soft and pretty!'

'I had to, Granny,' said Elizabeth. 'I did it with your nail scissors when I came one night to take Charles' riding-breeches to wear—and I took his jersey too, though it's so dirty now I don't expect he recognises it! Oh, Granny— I'm so very happy. You can't *think* how different I feel!'

'We'd better go,' said Peter to the others, in a low voice. 'Let's leave them all to be happy together. Come on, say good-bye.'

They said good-bye, and Scamper gravely shook paws as well. Then away they went on their bicycles, Scamper running beside them.

'What a wonderful finish!' said Jack. 'Who would have thought it would end like that? I feel rather happy myself! When's the next meeting, Peter?'

'Tomorrow—and we'll have a celebration to mark our success!' said Peter. 'Everyone must bring some food or drink. And we'll have to think of a new password, of course. What shall it be?'

'Stable-boy!' said Jack at once.

Well, it's quite a good one—but I mustn't tell you if it's the *right* one. Knock on the door of the shed, say 'Stable-boy!' and see if the Secret Seven let you in!